GHOOM

SOME RELATIONSHIPS ARE ETERNAL...

ANGAN CHAKRABORTY

I dedicate this book to my parents who never stopped me from doing things I love.

Contents

Prologue

Two kids are playing - a boy and a girl.

"Why should you always make tea for us? I can do it too," the boy complained.

"See, I am the wife, so I should be the one making it," said the little girl.

"No, today I'll make the tea and serve it. You take rest," the boy declared.

Amidst this playful bickering, a call was heard. "Rahuuuuul..." The little boy turned around.

CHAPTER ONE

Reminiscence

Rahul woke up with a jolt. Why did he see this dream? That too after so many years? He l leaned back on his bed and closed his eyes. Memories of distant childhood flashed before his eyes like a movie.

Rahul's father had transferable job due to which they never had a permanent home. Different cities had been their address over the time. But there was one place, where they had spent most of the time, that is Darjeeling.

During their stay there, they were acquainted with another bengali family. They too, were a family of three like Rahul's. Husband, wife and their daughter - Guriya, who was a little younger to Rahul. She was her only playmate, his friend, his partner-in-crime, his everything. They used to have frequent quarrels and fights too but were inseparable. The families used to meet each other frequently.

The year Rahul turned eight, his father got a transfer in Delhi. It was a sad news for everyone. The two families had bonded over the years. Now they would have to move to a new place, adjust with it accordingly. All again, from the scratch.

Guriya was crying uncontrallably the day they were leaving. They had come to see off Rahul and his family at the station. Little Guriya, in her mother's lap was looking literally like a doll. She kept looking at the train with watery eyes till it was out of sight.

Why this dream? Rahul could not shake off the thought. After staring blankly at the ceiling for some time, he decided that he will go to Darjeeling.

CHAPTER TWO

Mini-break

'Darjeeling?' Rahul's mother was surprised on hearing her son's sudden plan. 'Was thinking of going on a trip for a lot of days and this name popped in my head.' said Rahul. 'What a whimsical son I have!' retorted his mother.

Rahul is a freelancer by profession. So he wouldn't need any official permission before going on a trip. All he has to do is call up or send a message to his clients saying he won't be available for a few days and would resume his work after he returns. The best part was it was an off-season, so tickets and hotel bookings would not be an issue.

At 10:30 PM, Darjeeling Mail left the station. Rahul was overwhelmed by thoughts. Did he take the right decision? So many years have passed, does Guriya and her family still live there? What if they don't? She's not even that little kid anymore. Can she be called by the name 'Guriya' anymore? Will she recognise him? Do uncle and aunty remember him?

Rahul smiled. He connected his headphones to his phone and started listening to stories and dozed off in few minutes.

Cold winds woke him up from slumber. The trained had reached New Jalpaiguri (NJP). Now, it was only a matter of few hours and he would reach 'The queen of the hills' -

Darjeeling.

CHAPTER THREE

Journey

"First time in Darjeeling, Sir?" A question from the driver broke Rahul from his reverie. 'Hnuh?' he said.

"I'm asking, that is it your first time in Darjeeling, Sir?" the driver asked enthusiastically.

"Kind of.." said Rahul and leaned back into the seat.

"Then Sir, Tiger Hill, Ghum Monastery, Batasia Loop, Mall road, Tenzing Institute, The Zoo and ofcourse Keventer's and Glenary's....these are must," the driver said excitedly.

A smile came across Rahul's face. It's pretty evident that the driver knows every nooks and corner of the place. Every person here treats the whole place as their home and they love to give a tour of their home to others and why wouldn't that be?

One can fall in love with a place - this statement would not be understood by a person who has not visited Darjeeling.

The driver keeps talking but Rahul gets lost in his own thoughts. His own words resonates in his mind," The place you are mentioning about, I have been there, I have lived there. Maybe I don't remember it picture perfectly but this was my home too, once upon a time."

CHAPTER FOUR

The Search

After arriving at the hotel, Rahul freshened up and went for a walk at the mall road. He took a brief stop at Keventer's to buy a couple of sandwiches and a cup of coffee. Today, he would just roam around and relax a bit before he starts to look what he came for. Today, he would just inhale the essence of the place.

Rahul's mom had provided him with the address where they used to stay. On his way, a sudden thought came across his mind, Does the family still stay there? When they first shifted to Delhi, the mothers used to exchange letters but then life happened and the touch was lost. The last letter had come from the same address but eons have passed in between. "Let's see," Rahul said to himself. "Even if I don't get to meet her, atleast I'll get to enjoy a nice, peaceful trip." He consoled himself.

Sometimes, we don't like it when our thought come out to be true. A whole day passed but the people where nowhere to be found. Every person he met, failed to give the information he wanted. They do not stay there anymore, nobody knows their new whereabouts. Though Rahul had consoled himself earlier but still something broke down within. No matter how much he says that it is a trip after all but deep down he knows the reason behind it.

Returning back to the hotel, he picked up his phone and called the driver.

"Yes Sir!" The happiness was constant in the driver's voice.

"Hello. You were mentioning some places on our way to Darjeeling, would you able to take me to those spots tomorrow?" enquired Rahul.

"Sure Sir. I'll pick you up from a hotel at 3 A.M. Would that be okay Sir?" asked the driver. "Because if we don't leave early, you might miss the sunrise at Tiger hill Sir.."

"No. That won't be a problem, I'll inform my hotel manager." Rahul decided not to sleep. He knew himself very well, if he even closes his eyes, nobody will be able to wake him up.

Rahul laughed. 'Kumbhakarna' - a nickname his mother uses to address him at times, quite apt.

He kept on reading a book till Tamang, his driver arrived sharp at 3. He packed his bag with some necessory items and left for a whole day tour of Darjeeling.

At Tiger Hill, Rahul had a beguiling experience. People talk about the 'sunrise at Tiger Hill', but when the orange rays of the sun falls on the mighty yet elegant Kanchenjungha, it transports you to the different realm. It takes away all the worries and distress and fills the heart with unexplainable peace.

The rest of the sight-seeing was mesmerizing too. Rahul spent all his day, clicking pictures and chatting with Tamang. The day was well spent with memories captured in a camera and refreshing sights. His aim was to click so many pictures so that when he returns and revisits them, he would feel that he's still in Darjeeling.

Rahul spent the rest of his trip by roaming around the town. Walking through the roads without any particular destination, spending the evenings on a bench at the mall and having breakfast and evening coffee at Keventer's became a routine for him. Soon, it was time to bid farewell to the serenity, to go home.

CHAPTER FIVE

The Return

Rahul was at a station counter buying some chips and cake for the train journey when he felt someone was tugging his shirt. He looked around to see an adorable baby in his father's lap, smiling at him. He smiled back. Rahul made a funny face and the baby giggled.

The giggling made the baby's father turn around. He too was busy buying something. Rahul could not help but say,"Your kid is extremely adorable. Very friendly."

"Extremely naughty too.." The man smiled. "What's his name?" asked Rahul. Before the man could reply, a voice of a woman was heard." Have you finished buying cookies? The train's almost here."

"I was almost done but your son made a new friend in this short span.." The man said jokingly. Then he turned towards Rahul and said," Meet my wife, Ranjini." Ranjini and Rahul greeted each other.

"Let's complete the transaction by paying the shopkeeper..wouldn't want leave a bad reputation as tourists.." said the man while asking his wife to hold their baby. Rahul smiled at the jovial nature of the man.

After completing the payment, Rahul turned to the man,"Is this your first time here?" The man looked at Rahul with a mock terror in his eyes, "Absolutely not Sir, my wife loves mountains, you can call this our picnic spot. Her wish, my command." Saying this he looked at his wife, she smiled. Rahul was blown away by this simple yet lovable family. As they say, one can feel love if its geniune.

"Can I take a picture of your family?" Rahul asked. "Our picture!" The man looked surprised. Rahul said the truth,"Actually, I love the bonding you share, I have never seen such a beautiful family, touchwood."

"Alright, so where do we have to pose?" The man smiled. "Please stand here, I'll bring my camera." saying this Rahul rushed towards his bag.

While he was taking out the camera and adjusting the settings, he heard the man call out to his wife, "Guriya....can you and Rahul come here for a moment?"

The woman complained,"What are you doing? Calling me Guriya in front of so many people!"

"I'm extremely sorry, my lady. Actually it's become a habit. I have to say Ranjini very consciously." the man replied apologetically.

Till now, everytime he felt happy, Rahul's face had a smile. But at this very moment, his soul smiled. The trip did not disappoint. The last time he saw Guriya, she was in her mother's lap and today, after so many years, a little one was residing in her lap. The frame is exactly the same just the characters have changed.

"Smile!" Rahul clicked a picture. Then after adoring the little kid for sometime, he moved towards the train.

Darjeeling never lets anyone leave empty-handed,

9 798889 756408